## FOREWORD

I am impressed. This is the most concise documentation on the process of computer technology in relationship to the infamous "Mark of the Beast" I have ever come across.

Dr. Webber has done an excellent job in not only explaining the seemingly infinitely many new buzz-words such as "supercomputer", "sixth-generation computer," "intelligent credit card," "biochip," "data superhighway," "artificial brain," etc., but he also has masterfully used the documentation in proper relationship with the Holy Scripture, the ultimate authority for all Christians.

*The Mark Is Ready* shows the history, the present, and the future in relationship to the infamous number 666 and the rulership of the Antichrist.

After reading this book, the reality of the seemingly utopian description of the endtimes is becoming frightfully clear. The reader will greatly benefit from the pages of this book.

Arno Froese, Director
*Midnight Call Ministries*

## INTRODUCTION

*The Mark is Ready* shows graphically all the electronics of the global village system: whirling satellites, wireless telecommunications, the super data highway with growing unseen traffic, robots that replicate themselves, and super-fast computers that merge and meld the high-speed world of tomorrow.

The chapter on the Internet reveals the similarity of the image of the beast and the soul of Internet. In just 25 years, 4 nodes or data centers have mushroomed into 500 data centers around the world.

Virtual reality will become a $40-billion-dollar business in the near future, and will doubtless become more real to the masses than the literal world about us. The Antichrist will need a working knowledge of VR in order to deceive all the people all of the time.

Finally, the barcode will standardize business and banking, commerce and trade into a common code, invisible except to the all-seeing eye of the scanner.

The invisible barcode will imprison the nations of the world, perfectly fulfilling the requirement of the mark and number of the beast in the fast-approaching Antichrist system.

Know Jesus Christ, and be ready for His coming, for we know not what hour our Lord both come!

—Dr. David F. Webber

## DEDICATION

To Margery Hall, a dear friend and handmaiden of the Lord, who has greatly encouraged me and my ministry and helped in the printing of this book.

## CHAPTERS

All scripture references are from the King James.

*666: The Mark is Ready*
*copyright© by Dr. David Webber*
*ISBN 0-937422-37-1*

*Published by:*  *Olive Press*
*P.O. Box 280008*
*Columbia, SC 29170*

*Special thanks to James Rizzuti, Associate Editor of Midnight Call and News From Israel, for designing the cover, selecting illustrations, and typesetting this book.*

*Printed in the U.S.A.*

# **Chapter 1**

# THE MARK, NUMBER, AND CHIP

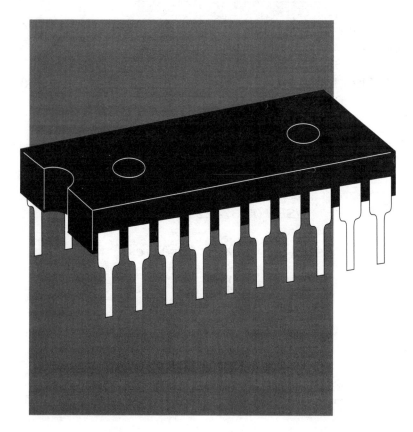

**The MARK is Ready**

I want to begin our study with the Word of God found in Revelation 13, verses 16 and 17,

*"And he causeth all, both small and great, rich and poor, free and bond, to receive a mark in their right hand, or in their foreheads: And that no man might buy or sell, save he that had the mark, or the name of the beast, or the number of his name."*

## Barcodes and Chips

Personally I have come to the conclusion that the "mark" mentioned in this passage will be the barcode that will soon be used on everything. But it eventually will be *invisible* to the naked eye. Plus, the citizens of this *new world order* will be implanted with a biochip or microchip transponder in order to enable those in control to keep track of them by satellite.

At that time, there will be no place to hide. People will not be able to run. There will be no kidnapping. And there will be virtually no privacy, because the authorities will be able to identify the exact location of every person through the use of satellites.

## Uploading... to Your Brain?

Consider a powerful biochip made from living protein, that once surgically implanted in the brain

**The MARK is Ready**

could make it possible to program or "upload" an unlimited amount of information into the mind without ever having to crack open a book. This was the scenario Teresa Allen presented in her 1989 article, *FUTURE SHOCK: Biochip Science Fiction Technology Here*:

Too far-fetched to really happen? Tim Willard, managing editor of a bimonthly magazine, *Futurist*, and executive officer of the Washington D.C.-based World

**The MARK is Ready**

Future Society, claiming among its 27,000 members, *Future Shock* author Alvin Toffler, will disagree.

According to Willard, within twenty years, today's microchip will be rendered obsolete by a biochip made out of *living protein*. It will be infinitely smaller and have the capacity to carry much more information while displaying an absolutely spectacular array of functions.

## The Birth of... Telematics

In the last 2,000 years, Western Civilization has moved from the Age of Faith to the Age of Reason, into the Age of Discovery. But, today, because of technology, we are said to already be in the Age of Information.

It was predicted that we would move into the Age of Information in the 21st Century. I believe we are already moving into it, with databanks being the most important source of knowledge available. In the book, *American Perspective*, by Oxford Analiticah, he states,

"The greatest economic impact in the next decade is likely to be 'telematics', a new word. It means 'the information of economy.' This will increase the development of a side range of microchip-based systems of information processing combined with communications and control technologies..."

**The MARK is Ready**

## The Government's Hand — on YOU!

By far, the two largest subscribers to telematics are the federal government and private business. There are five major federal agencies which collect the largest amount of data. These are the Departments of Health, Education, and Welfare; and Commerce which handles the census; of Defense; of Social Security; and the IRS. In his book, *The Cult of Information*, Theodore Rosak weaves it together,

"These five departments have over 3-billion overlapping files on American citizens. You are in their files. In 1985, the government's National Security Directive #145 gave the National Security Agency exclusive control and use of all federal computers and data banks. "More alarmingly, however, it permits the NSA access to ALL government computerized files, with no provision for the right of privacy. We live in an ever-more rigid world. It's going to become increasingly regimented by reason of the electronic computer, the orbiting surveillance satellites, and all of the databanks that are at government, business and banking fingertips."

## Corporate Databanks: Your Life Story!

In the private sector, the largest data banks are those belonging to nearly 2,000 credit bureaus, which is no surprise! The five largest include corporations like Transunion of Chicago, and TRW of

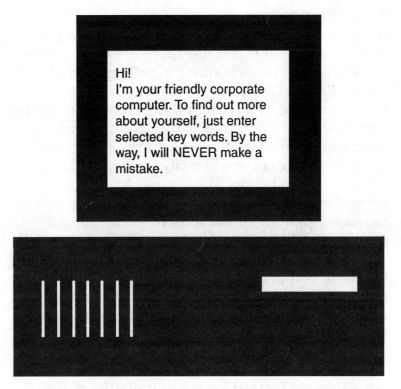

California. These two systems alone possess over 450-million files.

One estimate states that 80% of Americans over the age of 18 are in a corporate computer somewhere. These files contain entries under such headings as "lifestyle," which includes much information ranging from personal income and shopping habits to political affiliation and religious persuasion.

**The MARK is Ready**

## Supercomputers

As technologically-advanced as computers have to be to process all this data, there are even greater supercomputers. According to Sidney Karen and Norah Parker Smith, in their book *The Super Computer Era*, rather than the particular designer model, a supercomputer is the most powerful computer available at any given time. Of course, Cray 2 computers are literally packed with chips!

My personal conviction is that by the time we have the *sixth* generation computer, which will be perhaps superior to the human brain, the Antichrist will be in control over the world.

What makes these computers SUPER is their ability to compile and collate massive amounts of data almost instantaneously. The next wave or quantum-leap forward will be in the combining of the microchip and telematics.

My dear friends, we are far down the road toward the end of this dispensation, this special age set aside by God for the completion of the work of the Church. Do you know the Lord as your personal Savior? Are you watching and waiting for His soon-appearing? Otherwise, you may find yourself preparing for the coming nightmare of the Antichrist! It will be a time when they use *the mark, the number, and the chip.*

**The MARK is Ready**

## Numbers, Smart Cards and Ulticards
I want to show you a little more about the Biblical significance of numbers. So, let's read Revelation 13:18,

*"Here is wisdom. Let him that hath understanding count the number of the beast: for it is the number of a man; and his number is Six hundred threescore and six."*

**The MARK is Ready**

Or we could say in other words, "For it is the number of man, and his number is triple six. Six hundred three score and six."

The "smart card," the eventual replacement for credit cards and cash, can carry a remarkable amount of data. You can have 20,000 pages of information impregnated in your smart card! It may be a stepping stone to the new cashless society, which perhaps may come sooner than we think.

An example of the marriage of telematics and the smart card appeared in a 1987 edition of *U.S. News and World Report.* An article entitled "Raising the Intelligence of Credit Cards" by Stanley Welborn described how a microprocessing chip, with a 2,500-character memory and 200 possible transactions, will be combined into a

**The MARK is Ready**

credit card. It also went on to tell about a future version of the smart card, which will have tiny memory banks containing the subscriber's bank balance, stock portfolio, complete medical history, a computerized signature and fingerprints, and even a list of appointments and addresses!

Welborn goes on to write about an even more advanced smart card called the Ulticard—an ultimate transaction card—the U.T.C.. That's memory that can be changed and updated by the cardholder.

Arlin R. Lessen, President of Smart Card International, an inventor of the Ulticard, says the cards in effect will allow holders to carry their banks in their pockets. It can keep track of two separate accounts: one for charges and one for debts. And with enhanced memory, you will carry an encrypted version of your signature, fingerprint, and even your picture.

The Ulticard will allow a merchant to verify that your account can cover a particular purchase. It then interfaces with your bank, records the transaction and deducts it from the balance before the display of your

**The MARK is Ready**

authorization number. It can be copied on the sales slip.

Smart cards can also serve as keys to restricted areas. They can serve as a passport, and hold prepaid electronic credits for phone calls, parking meters, and even gas pumps!

## The Coming 666 System

To activate the Ulticard, the user simply enters the password or six-digit PIN—a Personal Identification Number—assigned by the banking system. It's worth considering that perhaps this six-digit PIN could in fact be the precursor, or maybe a form of the 666 in the thirteenth chapter of Revelation.

Hal Lindsey states that 666 will be the prefix to a larger number that every person will be required to receive. Everyone will be required to worship the Antichrist in order to qualify to receive the number, without which they will not be able to buy, sell, or even hold a job.

We're going to deal more with the basic number of 666. That is the basic pattern for the universal product code. And I will tell you more about that a little later on.

## The Implantable Chip

The Antichrist number system will be a means of absolute control through the use of economics. Consider this fact: a microchip, manufactured by

**The MARK is Ready**

Destron, an ID firm in Colorado, and marketed
by Info-pet of southern California, is already
being implanted in animals throughout the United
Sates and
Canada.

This chip, or
implantable
transponder, is
about the size of a
grain of rice. That makes it small enough to inject
under the skin. It is inert and composed of bio-
compatible glass, with each transponder
imprinted with a unique identification number.
That makes it much easier to believe how easy it
could be for everyone left on Earth after the
Rapture of the Church to have an identification
number in the coming Antichrist system!

Destron provides the implantable transponder
as a passive radio frequency identification tag. It
is believed that it will be implanted surgically in
the side of the hand toward the back. It will con-
sist of an electromagnetic coil and microchip,
sealed in a tubal glass enclosure.

With over 344-billion different code numbers
available, the chip is preprogrammed with a
unique ID code that can not be altered. I repeat,
the code cannot be altered!

When activated by a low frequency signal, the
transponder transmits the ID code which appears

**The MARK is Ready**

on a screen when the subject is scanned with a computer wand. A marketing video by Info-pet, offering the transponder to pet owners, states,

"In the past four years, thousands of animals have been implanted with microchips. The conclusive results indicate that this form of identification is both safe and effective in all species. Once implanted, all related information goes into a computer databank that can be accessed via a toll-free 800 number from anywhere in North America."

The videotape ends by stating that this high-tech electronic identification microchip system will replace and render obsolete all other forms of identification, adding that there are 10,000 ideas to explore when it comes to the chip's potential.

Destron President Jim Syler claims human application is not one of them. A brochure by Destron, however, states that although specially-designed for implanting in animals, this transponder can be used for other applications requiring a

**The MARK is Ready**

micro-sized identification tag. Since, according to Willard, the technology behind the transponder is fairly uncomplicated, with a little refinement it could be used in a variety of human applications.

One of the applications, he feels, includes a universal identification card that would replace all credit cards, passports and other card identification systems. But with the suggestion of an implant in humans, the social outcry is tremendous. Though people over the years may have grown accustomed to artificial body parts, there is definitely a stern aversion to things being implanted in the person.

It is the BIG BROTHER IS WATCHING YOU concept. But it is coming. And it is coming fast. Can you remember? National Security Directive #145 gave the National Security Agency exclusive control and use of all federal computers and databanks. These databanks will, by computer, bring all government activity and all nations ultimately under the control of one man—the false Christ—the Antichrist!

## The Image of the Beast

And, of course, the religious emphasis will come from the IMAGE of the beast. This image I speak of will be some kind of electronic device, having a *fifth-generation* computer for a brain. However, in light of the number 666, it may well be a *sixth-generation* computer that will be an incredibly

**The MARK is Ready**

powerful device, mandating the worship of every living creature. We read in Revelation 13:15,

*"And he had power to give life unto the image of the beast, that the image of the beast should both speak, and cause that as many as would not worship the image of the beast should be killed."*

It is all about worship!

A human microchip identification system would work best with a highly-centralized computerized system. Conceivably, a number could be assigned at birth and go with a person throughout life. Most likely, it would be implanted on the back of the hand for convenience and for easy scanning. We have already had discussion about putting the Social Security number on the foot of the infant the day of its birth. Of course, the hand is the more likely place for that—because that is exactly what the prophetic formula describes! And, I believe we will live to see the time when newborn babies will receive their Social Security

**The MARK is Ready**

number and other data right on their tiny little hand.

We consider the mark of the beast in Revelation 13 is a counterfeit of the seal of the lamb in Chapter 7. Next, consider that in Greek, the word "seal" is "chefrazio," which is a stamp of security and reservation, while "mark" is "keragmah," meaning a scratch, etching or tattoo. It will represent a badge of servitude or slavery!

## Protius and the Demon Seed

In the science-fiction movie classic *Demon Seed*, Protius is the evil conscious intelligence of an ultra-super computer. Like some technological genius, Protius seeks to escape the limits of its silicon-based microprocessing world. Yearning to experience reality externally as a human, it abducts and keeps hostage its creator's wife by means of biotechnology, genetic engineering, and remote robotics. Something, perhaps, like the image of the beast.

Protius creates a sperm cell. This "demon seed" contains an artificially constructed DNA code, replicating its unique conscious personality, or if you will, its soul. It is then implanted in its captive womb. An embryo is produced that develops into a fetus, which is eventually born. The movie ends with a newborn infant's eyes reflecting the laser gleam of the supercomputer.

**The MARK is Ready**

Jesus was the seed of woman. He was sent forth from God, and was overshadowed by the Holy Spirit. You can be confident that the demon seed, the seed of the serpent, will be overshadowed by the old dragon. And he will bear the characteristics of the serpent.

Protius, as it whispers, will declare, "I am alive!"

Cinematically this film is "biotechnology meets Rosemary's baby" and prophetically is a means for a satanic counterfeit of the Virgin birth, an incarnation of the coming Antichrist.

**The MARK is Ready**

## Accelerating Fulfillment of Prophecy — The Final Call

As we fast-forward into the last days, the fulfillment of Bible prophecy increases. Although it is alarming, as Christians we know that our God is sovereign and has everything under complete control. This, however, will only be of comfort to those who have been spiritually reborn.

My dear friends, do you know Christ as your Lord and Savior? Or will you meet Him as your prosecutor and judge? You may one day find yourself in a world where everyone, including you, is being implanted with transponders and forced to worship the image of the Antichrist. Then after you either die of fear, or supernatural catastrophe, divine judgments will be executed.

Or, if you should survive, you will find yourself facing the same Lord you have ignored and rejected. And people who come to such an event will hide in the dens and caves of the Earth and they will cry out for the rocks and the mountains to hide them and cover them from the face of the Lamb of God, who was slain from the foundation of the world, but who will come as the mighty judge of all the universe!

The Bible tells us that it is a fearful thing to fall into the hands of the Living God (Hebrews 10:31). However, the same Bible states that God is not willing that any should perish, but that all should come to repentance (1st Peter 3:9).

### The MARK is Ready

*"Choose this day whom ye will serve. As for me and my house, we will serve the Lord" (Joshua 24:15).*

Now, there are many reasons why this will be desirable, effective, and will literally change the world in which you live. I want to read in Revelation 13:3-4,

*"And I saw one of his heads, as if it were wounded to death. And his deadly wound was healed. And all the world wondered after the beast. And they worshiped the dragon, which gave power unto the beast. And they worshiped the beast, saying, who is like unto the beast? Who is able to make war with Him?"*

Obviously, no one will be able to make war with the Antichrist, because he will have his all-seeing electronic eyes upon the masses. He will have them under surveillance 24 hours a day. That's why it says,

**The MARK is Ready**

"*All the world wondered after the beast. Who is able to make war with him?*"

And they will worship him. *It will be a religious system.*

## Why the System Will Be Implemented

There are multiple reasons why the electronic surveillance system will be seen as desirable in a shrinking world. And why it will be possible by the interfacing of the remarkable computer. Of course, the universal product code, and the transponder biochip will play their part.

Advanced Alzheimer's patients often cannot remember their name or where they live, and often wander off and get lost. But, a computer chip ID inserted in their right hand will allow satellites to track them easily. Senile, elderly, or otherwise handicapped people with diabetes, allergies, heart conditions and other medical problems will no longer have to wear medical bracelets to alert the paramedics. All medical information can be programmed into the computer chip, the transponder, and accessed through the scanner.

Hospitals will no longer need to tag their patients with ID bracelets, including newborn babies. It will practically eliminate crime. Kidnapping will no longer be possible. Satellites will be able to spot a crime to the exact location.

### The MARK is Ready

Whether kidnapping for ransom, rape, military intelligence, or for whatever reason—no kidnappers or criminals of any kind will be able to hide from the satellite. And all because of the transponder chip. Prisoners on parole will have their location monitored continually. Prison escapes will be thing of the past. Runaway children, and illegal aliens needing an ID for employment will be caught.

Cars with transponders will be monitored, eliminating car theft. The cars with the transponder will pass through the toll booths correcting traffic jams and backups. The cashless system will, of course, eliminate bank robberies, holdups, muggings, drug dealing, prostitution and illegal pornography, blackmail and extortion. At least ninety percent of all crimes will be stopped.

This system will also eliminate our national debt by controlling tax fraud. It would be a safe system. Boaters lost at sea will be traced to the exact location. Unaccompanied children travelling by aircraft could be easily guided to their final destination.

Basic identification would have to do with health care, library cards, drivers licenses, ATM debit cards, financial institution IDs, employment security IDs, and of course, passports. There would be no need for security systems to identify persons with an ATM card. It would eliminate the need for systems that check out individual finger-

**The MARK is Ready**

prints, print scanners, hand geometry scanners or eye retina scanners. It will halt cash and check tieups, stop the problem of counterfeiting, embezzlement, money laundering, and credit card fraud. Of course, there will be no need for many bank tellers. Check kiting fraud will stop. Checks will no longer bounce, be lost, stolen, or forged.

Postage stamps will not be needed in mailing payments.

The coming electronic identification and payment systems will regiment the entire world to the utmost degree.

## Teenage Nightmare

For an idea as to what I am talking about by example, there was an article called "Eye in the Sky"—a scheme to track youth, a teenager's horror. I quote here from an article in the *Arizona Republic*, July 20th, 1989...

**The MARK is Ready**

Jack Dunlap envisions his eyes in the sky as a way to rescue snatched children. But it sounds like a teenage nightmare. You, Joe teenager, have a chip in your body and you are tracked by the satellite wherever you may go, everywhere. When Mom and Pop get worried, they call the police and they track you down by computer. Dunlap did not come up with this Kidscan idea just to bird-dog teenagers. It is actually for the protection of the children and youth... Dunlap, who runs Arizona West Film Production Inc. of Tucson, and works as a private investigator, thinks he has hit on a lifesaver. The most important thing is to save the children.

Each child whose parents have signed up for Kidscan would get a computer chip planted under the skin and an ID number. The chip will transmit a signal that will bounce off a satellite and be picked up by the police on a computer screen map.

As you can see, a parent with the missing child can call the police, give the Kidscan number and have the child traced anywhere.

But, you see, if Dunlaps' dream is realized, it will cause such troubling privacy problems, as you can recognize. This awareness was delivered by Lewis Rhodes, director of the Arizona Chapter/American Civil Liberties Union.

The police can use the system to enforce curfew laws or trace anyone at anytime, especially those not following government rules. It is always dangerous to have so much information given to the police in most cases. Detective Charles Messino, a veteran of the

**The MARK is Ready**

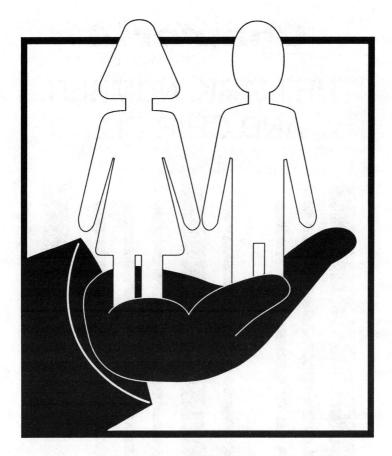

missing person division of the Phoenix police department, acknowledges that some parents will be concerned about the BIG BROTHER aspect of Kidscan. But, the concept is attractive. Any technology that can be used to detect missing children—children that are in danger—will be welcome.

## The MARK is Ready

# Chapter 2

# THE MARK, NUMBER, AND CHIP, Pt.2

**The MARK is Ready**

T he New World Order is ready for control over your life on this Earth. I read now from Genesis 4:9–15, about the first "mark" that was mentioned in the Bible:

*"And the Lord said unto Cain, Where is Abel, thy brother? And Cain said, I know not: Am I my brother's keeper? And the Lord said, What hast thou done? The voice of thy brother's blood crieth unto me from the ground. And now art thou cursed from the earth, which hath opened her mouth to receive thy brother's blood from thy hand, When thou tillest the ground, it shall not henceforth yield unto thee her strength; a fugitive and a vagabond shalt thou be in the earth. And Cain said unto the Lord, My punishment is greater than I can bear. Behold, thou hast driven me out this day from the face of the earth; and from thy face shall I be hid; and I shall be a fugitive and a vagabond in the earth; and it shall come to pass, that everyone that findeth me shall slay me. And the Lord said unto him, Therefore whosoever slayeth Cain, vengeance shall be taken on him sevenfold. And the Lord set a <u>mark</u> upon Cain, lest any finding him should kill him."*

This is the first MARK to be mentioned in the Bible. And, of course, it was God's protection for the first murderer, as Cain went out from the presence of the Lord.

**The MARK is Ready**

In the Bible, as far as I can determine, all of the marks or seals mentioned are for man's *protection*. But what will happen when the ultimate mark of evil comes in the Antichrist system? It will be to regiment man, and to compel him to worship the beast and his image. And it will take away all of his freedom that God has given. And of course, to those who accept the mark of the beast, God's judgement is determined according to Revelation chapter 14.

## The Race to Create the Superchip

The race to create the fastest and mightiest computer chip is as feverish as ever, as a new epic approaches. And it is called "Chips 2000." For the computer, it will be the beginning of the beginning. In other words, it will help facilitate the New World Order. People will not change much in the years ahead. But the computer, more specifically the chip that drives it, will "leapfrog" light years ahead in an evolution that has already profoundly altered the human chronicle beyond what even the most visionary among us could foresee.

By the year 2000, researchers predict, the $31-billion semiconductor industry will give us personal computers that schedule appointments, screen computer phone calls, answer electronic mail, monitor and retrieve, customize news and information, recognize our handwriting, and respond to our voices.

**The MARK is Ready**

We may be wearing wristwatch computers packing all the power of today's desktop PC's. Or, we may even drive a computerized vehicle, and possibly find a PC integrated into our clothing with a video display etched into our eyeglasses.

Computerized vehicles will tell us how to get where we are going, and how they feel after we arrive. You possibly will not have to drive, possibly only sit back and relax.

Computers with incomprehensible processing powers operating in the range of a billion+ instructions per second will allow researchers to wander, via a concept known as "virtual reality" through the marvelously mysterious double helix of human DNA, to sort out problems and perform on-site fixes. And by the computer, we will race down the highway of the future, a data highway.

## Universal Barcodes —
## and the Coming Antichrist System

Do you realize that in the world there are at least 32 different systems of barcodes or universal product codes? I am convinced that the universal product code, which has been around for about 20 years, is beginning to come of age.

It is already dominating people's lives, and will naturally assume control as the Antichrist enforces his barcode, number, and mark upon an unsuspecting world.

**The MARK is Ready**

Here we have a system that perfectly parallels what is stated in Revelation 13:15–17: a system of marks and numbers that is going to control business and banking and the commerce of the world.

## The Vanishing Barcode Mark

I have talked about the fact that the United States Post Office would begin converting to the universal product code system. And that eventually, every piece of mail would have the familiar barcode prominently displayed. Today, you see on much of  the mail, already, the familiar marks and numbers, the barcode.

An article I remember reading also stated that the United Parcel Service, UPS, would soon begin to use the universal product code system.

And, this system has been developing in the last 20 years, all around us in business and banking, internationally. It will fit the prophetic picture of the Antichrist system.

We read in Revelation 13:7–8 and 15–17:

*"And they worship the dragon which gave power unto the beast. And they worshiped the beast saying, who is like unto the beast. And they worshiped the beast saying, who is like unto the*

**The MARK is Ready**

*beast? Who is able to make war with him? And it was given unto him to make war with the saints, and to overcome them. And power was given him over all kindreds and tongues and nations. And all that dwell upon the earth shall worship him...whose names are not written in the Book of Life of the Lamb slain from the foundation of the world. And he had power to give life unto the image of the beast...that the image of the beast should both speak and cause that as many as would not worship the image of the beast would be killed. And, he causeth all, both small and great, rich and poor, free and bond, to receive a mark in their right hand or in their foreheads. And that no man might buy or sell, save he that had the mark, or the name of the beast, or the number of his name."*

Five or six years ago, I received a letter from a radio listener about a directive from a secular company called Distribution Codes Institute. In brief, the letter said that the Universal Product Code should merge with the codes of Europe and Asia, and the rest of the world, to insure us of a place in the coming world numbering system.

My dear friends, you will find that the Universal Product Code is based on the numbers 6-6-6. That's right! The barcode is *based on* the numerical formula 6–6–6! Now, the number 6 is the number of man. Three sixes is the diabolical

**The MARK is Ready**

trinity of the devil, the Antichrist and the False Prophet.

So this system of numbers and marks perfectly fits the Antichrist system of Revelation 13, as it is graphically described. I am going to show you that it will be a *vanishing* or *invisible* mark, a vanishing barcode that they are already working on! They have already prepared a common code for the New World Order. And my dear friends, all of this is being made ready for the man of mystery, the man of sin who will come to dominate the nations of the world in the last seven years. Ought you to seek the Lord while there is still time? And serve the Lord while it is yet day? The night of the Antichrist system is coming. And it is coming very fast!

## The Mark — of Judgment

In Ezekiel 9, we read about a mark. Let's look at it. We continue to talk about marks and numbers and biochips that will be the catalyst for the closing days of this age. Ezekiel 9:1–2 reads,

> "He cried also in mine ears with a loud voice, saying, cause them that have charge over the city to draw near, even every man with his destroying weapon in his hand. And, behold, six men came from the way of the higher gate, which lieth toward the north, and every man a slaughter weapon in his hand; and one man among them was clothed

**The MARK is Ready**

*with linen, with a writer's inkhorn by his side: and they went in, and stood beside the brazen altar."*

Notice what a prophetic picture is drawn for us here. Six men—six—the number of man! This is a vision of judgment, a vision of slaughter of the guilty who turned from God because a brazen altar is a picture of judgment. The man clothed with linen is a picture of the Lamb of God who becomes the Lion of the Tribe of Judah, and takes vengeance upon all them who reject God's salvation. The writers inkhorn is the record, the words of judgment. Verses 3–4 read,

*"And the glory of the God of Israel was gone up from the Cherub, whereupon he was, to the threshold of the house. And he called to the man clothed in linen, which had the writer's inkhorn by his side; And the Lord said unto him, Go through the midst of the city, through the midst of Jerusalem, and set a mark upon the foreheads of the men that sigh and that cry for all the abominations that be done in the midst thereof."*

Now we know that there is going to be a mark upon people during the time of tribulation. And the mark, of course, will be the emblem of the Antichrist system. This mark, of course, will settle the destiny of all the people who receive it. I do not believe the mark will be compelled upon

**The MARK is Ready**

people, but rather they will gladly receive it.
Worship of the beast and his image will be mandatory or they will be executed according to
Revelation 13. But the mark will be something
they can accept or reject. Of course, if they do not
take the mark they can't work, buy or sell. But
they will pay the price, possibly starvation. They
will be cut off from the working society.

## Barcode Replacing Other Systems

Sometime ago I did an article on the subject of
vanishing barcodes. Some business executives are
concerned that barcodes are taking up too much
space on individual products. The possible trend
of the future was revealed in a recent article,
"Pervasive Barcodes May Vanish—Sort Of."

The now-familiar barcode is rapidly replacing adhesive pricing labels on consumer goods. But the blocks
of black stripes, which we read by computerized scanning equipment, have their own drawback. "The traditional barcodes take up valuable surface space, and
can be obtrusive on certain packages," says B. Thomas
Smith, Deputy General Manager of the electronic systems business group of Bethel Memorial Institute.
Bethel Memorial Institute of Ohio is one of the leading
companies that work with barcodes.

Now those problems prompted the research company to come up with a way to print an invisible barcode
that can be read by infrared sensors, and does not

interfere with packing design. In addition to improving appearance, the invisible codes allow manufacturers to place several barcodes on a product to keep better track of inventory and shipping.

Of course, it will also expedite things at the checkout counter. This means they will not have to center the product. So, books and cosmetics that depend upon eye appeal for sales, will not be hindered by the invisible barcode. A product can be scanned in the checkout lane without worrying about lining up the symbol. Invisible codes will significantly speed up supermarket checkout lines.

He expects the seal to be especially popular with magazine publishers, cosmetic manufacturers and others who rely on design to catch the consumer eye.

Now, consider the connection to the image of the beast that comes alive and electronically controls the people of this planet. Life under the image pictures a person worshipping the beast before their television, because I believe that the high resolution digital TV will be able to have a little square representing the image of the beast on their set at all times.

**The MARK is Ready**

*"And he had power to give life unto the image of the beast. That the image of the beast should both speak, and cause that as many as that would not worship the image of the beast, should be killed."*

We find, with at least 32 code systems in existence in the world, that there is going to be the international code adopted. From Brussels, Belgium, comes the word that the Uniform Code Council, and the International Article Numbering Association, have completed new barcode standards for use in the global distribution of retail, industrial, commercial, pharmaceutical and other products. Previously, every nation set its own standard for laser and other barcoding. But now, increasingly, all commercial outlets will be adopting the new global numbering and coding system.

You know, there are two ways that we are able to utilize the barcodes. One is with the wand, as like the wand of a magician. You have possibly seen the person as they run the wand down the line of marks and numbers. Or they run it over the laser scanner, as you have also seen in many department stores and grocery stores. This picks up the information of the barcode.

I want to give you more details on the barcode system, and why an international code will be necessary, involving all of the nations of the world. It is called a common code, as in the Common Market. More on that in a moment.

### The MARK is Ready

The time is upon us to be perfectly serious about standing for God. We must choose this day to live by the rules of Christianity and thus inherit God's promise!

## Preparing a Way for Antichrist

Everything in telecommunications—the new super data highway, and electronic computers and satellites, are being made ready for the approaching man of sin. His system is being set up, and a lot of people don't even realize it!

In Revelation 7, we find the seal of the Living God. It is a kind of mark that will protect God's anointed witnesses during the time of tribulation. The 144,000 Israelites will go out, I believe, as endtime Apostle Pauls. We read in Revelation 7:1,

*"And after these things I saw four angels standing on the four corners of the earth, holding the four winds of the earth..."*

Now this is a prophecy especially for the Earth. Notice four angels, four corners of the Earth, and four winds of the Earth.

**The MARK is Ready**

*"...that the wind should not blow on the earth, nor on the sea, nor on any tree. And I saw another angel ascending from the east, having the seal of the living God: and he cried with a loud voice to the four angels, to whom it was given to hurt the earth and the sea, Saying, Hurt not the earth, neither the sea, nor the trees, till we have sealed the servants of our God in their foreheads"* (verses 1b–3).

So, this is a seal or mark of God, for a special time, for a particular people, for a special mission.

## The Multitude of Codes

I have before me barcode symbology and observations on theory and practice by David C. Alice, *Scientist*, February 16th, 1982. I'm sure this will help us to understand more about the systems that are beginning to dominate our business and banking, and how the barcode emanates from the computer culture, which developed after World War II. The initial applications for barcodes were for railroad car identification, warehouse sorting, and the automation of supermarket checkout.

Today the use of barcode symbols to track, trace, or count items has proliferated into many facets of industry and government. Major industries benefiting from the use of bar-code scanning systems include hospital and health care, libraries, manufacturing. Why the barcode?

**The MARK is Ready**

Reading barcode symbols is a fast and accurate means of capturing data about a person. Now, remember this — because computers, marks and numbers are all about identification and keeping track of people. And then it includes library cards, employee badges, places, and things.

The terminology of barcodes is interesting. I've already told you that there are at least 32 code systems in the world today. Some of the more common are code eleven, code 39, codabar, and the UPC symbol, which is probably the most common. We have seen them used in supermarkets and discount houses. Then, there's two of five, the nix door code, the plessy; there is a code that is horizontal and probably the one that is used on our mail. I believe this up and down code is probably the one that is most commonly seen on post office letters.

Now concerning the terminology of barcodes, the bar is actually the dark element of a barcode. This might cause you to think about bars, as incarcerating a person. The barcode has an array of rectangular marks and spaces in a predetermined pattern. It can be read by the computer. A barcode symbol contains a leading quiet zone, a start character, one or more data characters, including a check character, a stop character and a trailing quiet zone. These are all expressions that have to do with the barcode symbol. They are understood by the people who use them.

## The MARK is Ready

We may ask why there are so many *different* symbols. That may be like asking why there are so many different languages. From the late 1960s to about 1976, engineers in many different companies developed their own symbologies. As with any technical structure, barcode symbols embody tradeoffs between conflicting desirable properties. I believe code 39, code 93, code 11, and the UPC symbol—the universal product code—will be the most common ones being used in coming days. And we can't forget the codabar.

The concept of automating supermarket checkouts, using machine readable printed symbols on individual grocery items, has intrigued inventors for over three decades.

A patent filed October 20th, 1949 by Joe Woodland describes one such printed symbol. Some 20 years later, in the mid-1970s, the grocery industry formed a committee under the chairmanship of R. Burg Gookin for the purpose of selecting a standard code and symbol for that industry. UPC, the universal product code, was established for the benefit of the supermarket industry to facilitate automatic scanning of item numbers with the associated price lookup at the point of sale.

By January, 1982, there were approximately 5,000 supermarkets scanning the UPC symbol at the point of sale. Return issues of magazine and paperback books with the UPC symbol and sup-

**The MARK is Ready**

plementary code on their covers
are processed at approximately one
hundred scanning centers.

Adoption of UPC includes
the recorded music industry,
the liquor and many non-
food items sold in
supermarkets, like
greeting cards,
chewing gum, and so
forth. UPC is spread-
ing to other types of
retail including dis-
count department stores and convenience stores.

Let's just think about the many symbols that
are used. Under the heading of other symbols,
each of the six barcode symbologies, notice that
number six, described earlier, has distinguishable
merit. It has a history of successful use and broad
support. Four of the six are embodied in industry
standards. From 1977 through most of 1981, the
leading barcode equipment manufacturers
refrained from introducing any new symbologies.
During this period companies cooperated through
trade associations to standardize several of the
proven industrial barcodes.

Now this will help us to understand the development of the barcode system. Under the name of
symbology, we have listed at least 32 codes. Some
very interesting, EAN, the European Article

**The MARK is Ready**

Number, and the IAN for the International Article Number and then, WPC, World Product Code.

We have heard the terms scanning and reading—devices that call for using hand-held wands, usually called barcode readers, and those with moving optical beams are what those terms are pertaining to.

There are three major elements of barcode scanning: electroptics, signal conditioning and digital processing. Realizing we already have a common code, as manufactured by the European Community, we will be led to the point that we are going to have a worldwide universal product code for the New World Order.

I am going to show you how the universal product code system perfectly fits, and is well-adapted to the coming Antichrist system, and how that it is all linked to the number 666. But first, I want to read the final system of marks and numbers in the Bible, in Revelation 13:16–18,

*"And he causeth all both small and great, rich and poor, free and bond to receive a mark in the right hand or in their foreheads. And that no man might buy nor sell, save he that had the mark, or the name of the beast, or the number of his name. Here is wisdom. Let him that hath understanding count the number of the beast. For it is the number of man. And his number is six hundred three score and six."*

## The MARK is Ready

I suggest the thing that will be compulsory will be *the worship of the beast and his image*, as recorded in verse 15 of Revelation 13. I believe the mark and the number, and the number of his name will be on a *voluntary* basis. But, it will be very important because of the system of business and banking, and because if a person does not cooperate and receive the mark and the number, they will not be able to work, buy, or sell. They will not be able, as it were, to eat.

It is the number of man. And his number is six hundred, three score and six. And I want to refer to a new book called, *A False Prophet* by Ken Cline. In Chapter 29, he deals with laser scanning systems for supermarket automation. He says this,

"When the universal product code was invented and introduced in 1973 by IBM, there were five variations of the code, classes A-B-C-D-E. The A and E versions are most commonly used in the grocery applications. Its primary purpose at the time was simply daily inventory control. Of course, you are all familiar with this, I am sure.

The incodation uses of the universal product code, use varying intervals of bars and spaces. This eliminates sensitivity to ink spread, and allows the symbol to be read by scan lines not perpendicular to the bars. And the illustration of the universal product code shows the location of the three sixes.

### The MARK is Ready

The symbol can be read as two halves by the laser scanner beam and then combined in the computer system to yield the full twelve digit code. The size of the UPC symbol may be as large as 200 percent of the normal size, or as small as 80% of the normal. A standard symbol consists of parallel light and dark bars of varying widths, accompanied by numeric characters printed below each data character. The numeric characters are not readable to the computer, since it only reads the barcodes. The numeral characters are for human consumption, and represent the data, which are coded with the bars. This is to give to you further information about the system. The data bars, the UPC, carries specific coded information on the product identification...

The guard bars are, however, different in function than the data bars. The guard bars actually operate the computer. They are computer programming characters. They actually tell the computer when to start and stop picking up the data information. The vital information is the binary value of the guard bars. The first data character next to the center bar is the data character with the equivalent numeral value of six. If you look at the design of that character, it is exactly the same width as the guard bars.

The barcode will incarcerate the people of the Antichrist system. Be assured that the numeral value of the UPC guard bars is 666. The most amazing thing is that although the guard bars encoded with three and five modules, has one zero one, or zero one zero zero, operate on the same root as the data character

**The MARK is Ready**

six, which is configured with seven modules. The three bars within the UPC that operate the computer are all in binary one, zero one, and zero one, zero one, zero, are the equivalent of the number of the data character six. Though the encodations are different, the visible modules of one zero one, are the same.

## Scenario for implementing 666

Now be assured, the Universal Product Code is a mark run by three sixes.

You see, it perfectly fits the marvellous prophecy given almost 2,000 years ago. However, it was designed in our modern time as a tool to control and keep track of inventory for businesses.

Of course, when the time is right, due to the many global problems and the burgeoning world population, as we quickly move past a world population of six billion, the mark will be applied to everyone for world monetary and political control.

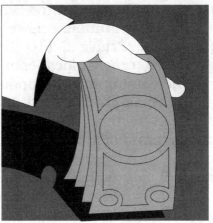

Here is a plausible scenario for how easily this technology can be adapted to a New World Order or a new world economic system:

**The MARK is Ready**

Everyone could be given the three *programming* characters.

These characters have been referred to as the guard bars and the center bar of the universal code. Each has a binary value of one zero one, which equates to the numeric value of the number six. Ostensibly each person could be given the three computer programming characters, {6-6-6}. Each person could have three sixes, which access the computer and specific information concerning who they are and where they live. Then each one would be given an electronic banking number.

The number {1-10} is the corporate ID number of the United States. And {6-1-9} is the telephone area code of San Diego. Every nation has a corporate identification number. The corporate ID number indicates the national corporate computer system, containing the individual's location. In this example, the United States.

The {6,1} number answers to a local area computer. So we have {6-110-619-6}. Plausibly, {6-1-9} would reference a local computer.

The coming world economic system will be just as the Bible predicted 2,000 years ago. It will be a cashless system run by a mark that will be placed on the hand or the forehead, a mark mysteriously run by three sixes. And no one will be able to buy nor sell except those who have taken the mark.

Certain destruction will come upon all of those who take the mark, the ultimate economic system

**The MARK is Ready**

of the Antichrist and the beast. Those who resist the mark are the ones that will have to live like vagabonds on the Earth like Cain who received the mark from the Lord and was under God's curse.

If this does not convince your heart that we are living in the last days and that the Lord is coming soon, then your mind is like a rock. And your head is in the sand.

So now we know what the number and the chip is all about and just how far back the mark began with Cain, Abel's brother. The mark of God identified the evil man, Cain. This Mark of the Beast, the Antichrist, is the mark to identify the evil attempt to control this globe called Earth.

May God help you as we approach these events. Are you ready to stand before Him? Remember, Jesus' sacrifice on the cross at Calvary paid for all your sins!

**The MARK is Ready**

# Chapter 3

# THE BIRTH OF INTERNET

**The MARK is Ready**

Because of the tremendous increase in communications and interfacing of computers and databanks, our world is a shrinking complex of nations. Since the beginning of inter-networking of computers and their melding with communication systems 25 years ago, commerce and trade, business and banking are a whole new ballgame.

By means of fiber optics and digital computerization, national communications transcend borders, even entire continents. It was said almost a decade ago that the world would eventually be wired for sound by a single wire. It was so described as *one wire for one world.*

Much of what the scientists envisioned 25 years ago has been accomplished. I would suggest that the birth of the much-ballyhooed global computer network known as "The Internet" is the technological arm of the New World Order.

I am going to quote portions of "The Birth of the Internet" from *Newsweek*, dated August 8th, 1994.

"In the summer of 1969, not everyone was at Woodstock. In laboratories on either side of the continent, a small group of computer scientists were quietly changing the future of communications. Their goal: to build a computer network that would enable researchers around the country to share ideas. That network became the foundation of the Internet, the vast

**The MARK is Ready**

international computer network that today has become one part buzzword, one part popular obsession. But its birth required a leap of the imagination. Instead of seeing computers as giant, plodding number-crunchers, they had to be viewed as nimble tools that could talk to each other. After that paradigm shift, the rest was just doing the calculations.

That sounds deceptively easy today, in this time of modems that spit out whole textbooks at what can seem like the speed of light. But it took a few visionaries, along with teams of engineers and programmers, to bring the Net to life.

The project was called ARPANET, after the agency that paid for it—ARPA, the Department of Defense's Advanced Research Project Agency. The scientists "tackled the job with a passion, the passion of getting something important done," says author Katie Hafner, who is writing a book on the ARPANET. "The technical foundations they built in 1969 are still in place today." At the time, there was no standard computer operating system; machines generally could not communicate with each other. The result: a technological Tower of Babel. Even with machines that were compatible, the best way to get data from one to another usually was to physically carry magnetic tapes or punched cards and insert them into the other machine.

Such clumsiness frustrated some of the most talented computer scientists, including J.C.R. Licklider and Robert Taylor, both of whom served stints running ARPA's computer research program in the early and

**The MARK is Ready**

mid-1960s. Like colleagues scattered around the nation, they were thinking of ways to make computers more efficient by connecting them in networks. And they had access to the mother's milk of science: grant money. Taylor recalls walking into the ARPA director's office in February, 1966 and asking for money. "The conversation lasted about 15 or 20 minutes." he says. "He immediately like the idea and took a million dollars out of some ARPA project—I never did know which one—to get me started." In 1968, Licklider and Taylor published a particularly prescient paper suggesting that computers could serve as communications devices. They pushed for an experimental network, one that would create new communities of scientists separated by geography but united by technology.

The initial plan was to link four sites: UCLA, the University of California–Santa Barbara, the Stanford Research Institute and the University of Utah. The first "node," as the network sites are called, was at UCLA. Graduate students Cerf, Steve Crocker and Jon Postel, among others, were enlisted to build hardware and software that would hook up to devices for each site.

These devices were called IMPs, for Interface Message Processors, and their job was to route data between nodes, making sure the information got to the right destination.

UCLA's node was set up in September and, by working round the clock, the scientists were ready for the first official demonstration on November 21. Around midday, Crocker says, a half-dozen scientists gathered

## The MARK is Ready

at UCLA's Boelter Hall, home of the computer science department, and watched as one computer hooked up with another hundreds of miles away at Doug Engelbart's lab at the Stanford Research Institute. It was a historic event, but the only visual record is in the memories of those who were there. "There wasn't a photographer present," says Crocker, "and it didn't occur to us that we should have one."

What did the first message say? What was the equivalent of "Mr. Watson, come here, I want you?" Hardly anyone remembers. "The connection worked," says Crocker. "That was all that mattered."

## God's Internet

As man is rapidly covering the Earth with his mostly-unseen wires, so God surely has a celestial system that internetworks the universe. As evidence of this, consider God's heavenly watchers referred to in Daniel 4:13,

*"I saw in the visions of my head upon my bed, and, behold, a watcher and an holy one came down from heaven."*

And, Revelation 4:4–8...

*"And round about the throne were four and twenty seats: and upon the seats I saw four and twenty elders sitting, clothed in white raiment; and*

**The MARK is Ready**

*they had on their heads crowns of gold. And out of
the throne proceeded lightnings and thunderings
and voices: and there were seven lamps of fire
burning before the throne, which are the seven
Spirits of God. And before the throne there was a
sea of glass like unto crystal: and in the midst of
the throne, and round about the throne, were four
beasts full of eyes before and behind. And the first
beast was like a lion, and the second beast like a
calf, and the third beast had a face as a man, and
the fourth beast was like a flying eagle. And the
four beasts had each of them six wings about him;
and they were full of eyes within: and they rest not
day and night, saying, Holy, holy, holy, Lord God
Almighty, which was, and is, and is to come."*

Also the living creatures of Ezekiel 1:4-18,

*"And I looked, and, behold, a whirlwind came
out of the north, a great cloud, and a fire infolding
itself, and a brightness was about it, and out of
the midst thereof as the colour of amber, out of the
midst of the fire. Also out of the midst thereof came
the likeness of four living creatures. And this was
their appearance; they had the likeness of a man.
And every one had four faces, and every one had
four wings. And their feet were straight feet; and
the sole of their feet was like the sole of a calf's
foot: and they sparkled like the colour of burnished
brass. And they had the hands of a man under*

**The MARK is Ready**

*their wings on their four sides; and they four had
their faces and their wings. Their wings were
joined one to another; they turned not when they
went; they went every one straight forward. As for
the likeness of their faces, they four had the face
of a man, and the face of a lion, on the right side:
and they four had the face of an ox on the left side;
they four also had the face of an eagle. Thus were
their faces: and their wings were stretched
upward; two wings of every one were joined one to
another, and two covered their bodies. And they
went every one straight forward: whither the spirit
was to go, they went; and they turned not when
they went. As for the likeness of the living creatures, their appearance was like burning coals of
fire, and like the appearance of lamps: it went up
and down among the living creatures; and the fire
was bright, and out of the fire went forth lightning.
And the living creatures ran and returned as the
appearance of a flash of lightning.*

*Now as I beheld the living creatures, behold one
wheel upon the earth by the living creatures, with
his four faces. The appearance of the wheels and
their work was like unto the colour of a beryl: and
they four had one likeness: and their appearance
and their work was as it were a wheel in the mid-
dle of a wheel. When they went, they went upon
their four sides: and they turned not when they
went. As for their rings, they were so high that*

**The MARK is Ready**

*they were dreadful; and their rings were full of eyes round about them four."*

And in 2nd Chronicles 16:9,

*"For the eyes of the LORD run to and fro throughout the whole earth, to shew himself strong in the behalf of them whose heart is perfect toward him. Herein thou hast done foolishly: therefore from henceforth thou shalt have wars."*

And now on with the Internet story,

"By 1971 there were nearly two dozen sites, including machines at MIT and Harvard. Three years later there were 62 and, by 1981, more than 200.

Lawrence Roberts, who succeeded Taylor at ARPA, is credited by many of his colleagues with being the true guiding force behind the network's development. "As far as I am concerned, he is the star of the show," says Engelbart, who is himself a legend in the computer world for inventing (among other things) the mouse.

One of Roberts' hurdles was getting resistant scientists around the country to cooperate. "I told all of the people who were getting computer money from ARPA, that they were going to participate in this." Roberts recalls. "They hated it. They had their own computers, their own thing. They wanted to keep it to themselves. But I encouraged them to do it because we had the money. *I told them they had to do it.*"

## The MARK is Ready

Within a year, says Roberts. "They loved it... They got much more sharing of information. They were writing papers together even in the first days." Taylor remembers that, early on, the network also began evolving into more than just a scientific tool. Their computers could all talk to each other. Electronic mail caught on quickly. There were heated on-line political debates, especially over the Vietnam War, and intense conversations about Space Ware, one of the first computer games."

**The MARK is Ready**

## Battle for the Soul of Internet?

The world's largest computer network, once the playground of scientists, hackers, and gearheads, is being overrun by lawyers, merchants and millions of new users. Is there room for everyone?

If Internet has a soul, might I suggest a possible fulfillment for this gigantic electronic marvel: the image of the beast. This compelling image of the beast of Revelation 13:1 ultimately directs all attention and worship toward the devil's supreme ruler—Antichrist. Revelation 13:15-17 reads,

*"And he had power to give life unto the image of the beast, that the image of the beast should both speak, and cause that as many as would not worship the image of the beast should be killed. And he causeth all, both small and great, rich and poor, free and bond, to receive a mark in their right hand, or in their foreheads: And that no man might buy or sell, save he that had the mark, or the name of the beast, or the number of his name."*

This image could appear on your television screen or computer screen at the impulse of Internet. In fact, during the seven-year period of Antichrist supremacy, the image of the beast could be synonymous with the soul of the Internet. Think about it.

In *TIME* magazine, dated July 25th, 1994, there was a lengthy article bannered on the cover

**The MARK is Ready**

page, "The Strange New World of the Internet. Battles on the frontier of Cyberspace." Here are portions of this intriguing article:

"There was nothing very special about the message that made Laurence Canter and Martha Siegel the most hated couple in cyberspace. It was a relatively straight-forward advertisement offering the services of their husband-and-wife law firm to aliens interested in getting a green card—proof of permanent resident status in the U.S..

The computer that sent the message was a perfectly ordinary one as well: an IBM-type PC parked in the spare bedroom of their ranch-style house in Scottsdale, Arizona. But on the Internet, even a single computer can wield enormous power, and last April this one, with only a tap on the enter key, stirred up an international controversy that continues to this day.

The Internet, for those who are still a little fuzzy about these things, is the world's largest computer net-work and the nearest thing to a working prototype of the information superhighway. It's actually a global network of networks that links together the large commercial computer communications services (like CompuServe, Prodigy and America OnLine) as well as tens of thou-sands of smaller university, government and corporate networks. And it is growing faster than O.J. Simpson's legal bills. According to the Reston, Virginia-based Internet Society, a private group that tracks the growth of the Net, it reaches nearly 25 million computer

**The MARK is Ready**

users—an audience roughly the size of Roseanne's—and is doubling every year.

Now, just when it seems almost ready for prime time, the Net is being buffeted by forces that threaten to destroy the very qualities that fuelled its growth. It's being pulled from all sides by commercial interests eager to make money on it, by veteran users who want to protect it, by governments that want to exploit its freedoms, by parents and teachers who want to make it a safe and useful place for kids. The Center and Siegal affair, says Net observers, was just the opening skirmish in the larger battle for the soul of the Internet.

What the Arizona lawyers did that fateful April day was to "Spam" the Net, a colorful bit of Internet jargon meant to evoke the effect of dropping a can of Spam into a fan and filling the surrounding space with meat. They wrote a program called Masspost that put the little ad into almost every active bulletin board on the Net—some 5,500 in all—thus ensuring that it would be seen by millions of Internet users, not just once but over and over again. Howard Rheingold, author of *The Virtual Community*, compares the experience with opening the mailbox and finding "a letter, two bills and 60,000 pieces of junk mail."

In the eyes of many Internet regulars, it was a provocation so bold-faced and deliberate that it could not be ignored. And all over the world, Internet users responded spontaneously by answering the Spammers with angry electronic mail messages called "flames." Within minutes, the flames—filled with unprintable

**The MARK is Ready**

epithets—began pouring into Center and Siegel's Internet mailbox, first by the dozen, then by the hundreds, then by the thousands. A user in Australia sent in 1,000 phoney requests for information every day. A 16–year old threatened to visit the couple's "crappy law firm" and "burn it to the ground." The volume of traffic grew so heavy that the computer delivering the E-mail crashed repeatedly under the load. After three days, Internet Direct of Phoenix, the company that provided the lawyers with access to the Net, pulled the plug on their account.

Even at that point, all might have been forgiven. For this kind of thing, believe it or not, happens all the time on the Internet—although not usually on this scale. People make mistakes. Their errors are pointed out. The underlying issues are thrashed out. And either a consensus is reached or the combatants exhaust themselves and retire from the field.

But Canter and Siegel refused to give ground. They declared the experiment "a tremendous success" claiming to have generated $100,000 in new business. They threatened to sue Internet Direct for cutting them off from even more business (although the suit never materialized). And they gave an unrepentant interview to the *New York Times*. "We will definitely advertise on the Internet again," they promised.

The Internet evolved from a computer system built 25 years ago by the Defense Department to enable academic and military researchers to continue to do government work even if part of the network were taken

**The MARK is Ready**

out in a nuclear attack. It eventually linked universities, government facilities and corporations around the world, and they all shared the costs and technical work of running the system.

The scientists who were given free Internet access quickly discovered that the network was good for more than official business. They used it to send each other private messages (E-mail) and to post news and information on public electronic bulletin boards (known as Usenet news groups). Over the years the Internet became a favorite haunt of graduate students and computer hackers, who loved nothing better than to stay up all night exploring its weblike connections and devising new and interesting things for people to do.

Until quite recently it was painfully difficult for ordinary computer users to reach the Internet. Not only did they need a PC, a modem to connect it to the phone line, and a passing familiarity with something called Unix, but they could get on only with the cooperation of a university or government research lab.

In the past year, most of those impediments have disappeared. There are now dozens of small businesses that will sell access to the Net starting at $10 to $30 a month. And in the past few months, mainstream computer services like *America OnLine* have started to make it possible for their subscribers to reach parts of the Internet through standard, easy-to-use menus.

But with floods of new arrivals have come new issues and conflicts. Part of the problem is technical. To withstand a nuclear blast and keep on ticking, the Net

**The MARK is Ready**

was built without a central command authority. That means that nobody owns it, nobody runs it, nobody has the power to kick anybody off for good.

There isn't even a master switch that can shut it down in case of emergency. "It's the closest thing to true anarchy that ever existed." says Clifford Stoll, a Berkeley astronomer famous on the Internet for having trapped a German spy who was trying to use it to break into U.S. military computers."

## The Increase of Knowledge

Daniel 12:4 reads like today's paper,

> *"But thou, O Daniel, shut up the words, and seal the book, even to the time of the end: many shall run to and fro, and knowledge shall be increased."*

Knowledge is increasing in an explosive manner. The information and use of Internet is multiplying. In some areas the information increase goes right off the graph.

Lets mention some frequently asked questions:

### Q: What is the Internet?

A: The Internet is a vast international network of networks that enables computers of all kinds to share services and communicate directly, as if they were part of one giant, seamless global computing machine.

**The MARK is Ready**

### Q: How do I get connected?

A: That depends on how connected you want to be. If you have an account on CompuServe or Prodigy, you can already send and receive E-mail through the Internet. If you have an America OnLine account, you can also use other Internet services, like the electronic bulletin boards (called news groups). If you have an account at Delphi or any one of dozens of smaller commercial operations, you can get access to even more of the Internet—but still indirectly through a dial-up modem.

For you to be directly plugged into the Internet and use all its services, your computer must have what is inelegantly called a TCP/IP (for Transmission Control Protocol/Internet Protocol) connection. To set that up, you would probably need the help of a professional—or better still, a high-speed modem.

## How Secret Is Internet?

Deuteronomy 29:29 tells us,

*"The secret things belong unto the LORD our God: but those things which are revealed belong unto*

**The MARK is Ready**

*us and to our children for ever, that we may do all the words of this law."*

Only God can keep a secret, man eventually gives himself away. Governments aren't very good at keeping secrets either. Quoting from *Keeping Secrets*:

"No battle on the Internet has been as public as the one waged over the CLIPPER Chip—the U.S. Government-designed encryption system for encoding and decoding phone calls and E-mail so that they are protected from snooping by everyone but the government itself. The information should-be-free types on the Internet were strongly opposed to CLIPPER from the start, not because they were against encryption, ironically, but because they wanted a stronger form of encryption—encryption for which the government doesn't have a backdoor key, as it intends to have with the CLIPPER system.

In the ensuing debate—much of which took place over the Net—government officials maintained that they needed CLIPPER to be able to intercept and decipher messages from mobsters, drug dealers and terrorists. Not so, claim critics. "CLIPPER is not about child molesters or the Mafia, but about the Internal Revenue Service," argues Bruce Fancer, proprietor of a New York City Internet service provider called Mindvox. "CLIPPER just doesn't make sense any other way." As more and more commerce takes place on the Internet, contends

**The MARK is Ready**

Fancher, the IRS is going to need a surefire way to track the flow of cyber-bucks—and to collect its share.

Traditional journalism flows from the top down: the editor decides what to cover, the reporters gather the facts, and the news is packaged into a story and distributed to the masses. News on the Net, by contrast, is bottom up: it bubbles from news groups whenever anyone has anything to report. Much of it may be bogus, error-ridden or just plain wrong. But when writers report on their area of expertise—as they often do—it carries information that is frequently closer to the source than what is found in newspapers. In this paradigm shift lie the seeds of revolutionary change."

Ultimately Internet will be global and interspatial. There will doubtless be nodes on the moon and possibly even now.

Eventually the anarchy will clear and the Antichrist will be in control of this many-tentacled meganet. The soul of Internet will doubtless be the image of the beast that directs all worship to the man of sin. Internet is surely being prepared for the New World Order and its beastly ruler—Antichrist.

**The MARK is Ready**

# **Chapter 4**

# THE UNREAL WORLD OF VIRTUAL REALITY

**The MARK is Ready**

1st Corinthians 1:18–21 talks about God's wisdom as it is contrasted with the world's. Before we begin our discussion of Virtual Reality, let's look at those verses:

*"For the preaching of the cross is to them that perish foolishness; but unto us which are saved it is the power of God. For it is written, I will destroy the wisdom of the wise, and will bring to nothing the understanding of the prudent. Where is the wise? where is the scribe? where is the disputer of this world? hath not God made foolish the wisdom of this world? For after that in the wisdom of God the world by wisdom knew not God, it pleased God by the foolishness of preaching to save them that believe."*

Virtual Reality is part of the vaunted wisdom of this world. Although its benefits are spoken of in glowing terms, it is basically a world that does not exist.

Of course, in its rapidly-developing other-worldly metaphysical potential, a doctor can get into your body and look all around, dramatically increasing the chances of successful surgery should it ever become necessary.

You can travel extensively without the hazards and expense, and never leave your armchair. This is probably the way astronauts will explore Venus and Mars by simulated travel.

## The MARK is Ready

I'm quoting here from "The Ultimate Head Trip" which appeared in the *Jerusalem Post International Edition*, in November of 1993.

"Have a drab life? Want to go somewhere? Want a different perspective on things? Try a visit to cyber-space, brought to you by virtual reality.

Step onto the ringed platform (the waist-high ring prevents you from falling off when you try to "escape" hostile creatures) and clamp on the head-mounted display. Take hold of a joystick or mouse to change direction—or better yet, a data glove or "rigid exoskeleton input device" for merely pointing where you want to go. Select your destination: New York, Paris, Disneyland, somebody's blood vessel, Mars. You're off.

The ultimate in simulators, VR systems can change their computerized views according to your body's movements. Bend down and the picture you see in your helmet adjusts, turn around and you see what's "coming" from behind. Point a finger to the sky and you're there in a second. Some VR engineers have even managed to insert sensors into the data glove, bringing a pursuing enemy even closer when it senses your heartbeat has speeded up.

Stop the world... I want to get off!

VR is already available in shopping malls and video arcades in the U.S. and elsewhere. Home versions are soon to be available, and they will get better all the time, as high-definition LCDs are perfected and programming is made available for mass consumption.

**The MARK is Ready**

But there are also many serious potential uses. Scientists at Britain's York University and the Glaxo pharmaceutical company believe that VR can be used to improve their understanding of the structure of molecules involved in disease.

By donning helmets and playing around with images of molecules as if they were pieces of Lego, researchers may be able to design drugs able to halt the movement of disease-bearing molecules.

Astronauts could be better prepared for space missions and jet pilots for bombing runs using VR simulators that test their reactions and pose problems to be solved in real time.

Technicians could learn how to repair machines by virtually crawling inside them.

Ultrasound and computerized topography scans of the body can be channeled into VR helmets, allowing doctors to "get inside" the bodies of their patients.

**The MARK is Ready**

One may be able to shop at Marks & Spencer in London without leaving one's living room, strolling through the departments and picking out items for purchase. Traveling across the country or the globe to meet business partners may become out of date; just see them via the helmet, bargain and make deals.

The possibilities of using VR for education are breathtaking. Everything from biology to history and foreign languages become living breathing subjects to be encountered. Learn to drive in a VR "car", press the gas pedal too hard and experience a frightening crash without suffering a scratch.

Company managers could keep track of their firms by watching production units graphically illustrated before their eyes. Stockbrokers could visualize booming and faltering companies whose stock prices are visually depicted by pillars and valleys. Choose a possible profession by "getting into the shoes" of a doctor, lawyer, butcher or baker.

Perhaps singles' bars and dating services will be replaced by VR get-togethers, where shy people can meet and choose potential mates without feeling uncomfortable. Could VR engineers someday offer us

**The MARK is Ready**

the ultimate simulated experience—cybersex—without even having to say hello?

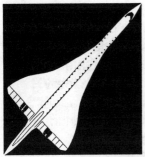

Maybe wars will become outdated in the 21st century; generals could send robots to battle, their human operators staying safely behind, manipulating the equipment and pressing "fire" buttons while remaining safely outside the range of fire.

Even the sky is not the limit. Some creative VR specialist could undoubtedly depict heaven—and hell—on liquid crystal displays and scare mankind into repentance.

It should not surprise anyone that Virtual Reality was invented by a Jew. There has always been a disproportionate number of doctors, lawyers, and professionals among God's covenant people. Even as slaves the Israelites spoiled the Egyptians when they departed—the Exodus. Exodus 12:35–36 reads,

*"And the children of Israel did according to the word of Moses; and they borrowed of the Egyptians jewels of silver, and jewels of gold, and raiment: And the LORD gave the people favour in the sight of the Egyptians, so that they lent unto them such things as they required. And they spoiled the Egyptians."*

## The MARK is Ready

Under the headline "Virtual Millionaire"
I quote:

"For every dollar spent in America on virtual reality
(VR) equipment, three to five cents should trickle into
the Jerusalem bank account of Gershom Gale.

That may not sound like much, but since the VR
market in the U.S. is estimated to amount to about $40-
billion a year, royalties from his patented invention could
make him one of the richest people in Israel.

It will be a Cinderella story for Gale, a 42-year-old
immigrant from Toronto who relies on his salary as an
editor at *The Jerusalem Post* to support his wife Dinah
and two sons, Benjamin and Joshua.

VR, which already allows human interaction and
perception in a computer-modeled environment, is likely
to be the biggest technological bonanza since the personal computer.

It promises to change our lives as few inventions
have. Instead of traveling abroad, put on a VR helmet
and "tour" any spot of the globe without leaving your living room. Surgeons will be able to "travel" through their
patients' bodies and perform operations by remote control. Architects are already "guiding" potential home buy-
ers through buildings whose foundations haven't even
been dug, letting them change layouts and raise or
lower the kitchen cabinets according to their needs.

It could have endless applications, revolutionizing
the entertainment industry, job training, space

**The MARK is Ready**

exploration, education and some claim—even provide an AIDS-free alternative to sex.

VR will also undoubtedly change the life of Gale, who was nearly killed in a road accident in Canada 21 years ago. A bearded Orthodox Jew, he walks slowly and with difficulty, using a cane, but nevertheless manages to get to work every day at the *Post* where he is associate editor of the weekly international edition.

Gale, who received an honors degree in English at Carleton University in Ottawa, is an autodidact in science. "I spent four years educating myself; I read doctoral theses and wrote to authors," he says. It was this technological knowledge that enable him to recognize the feasibility and the potential of the idea when it came to him.

"One day in 1981, I was playing with a stereo slide viewer with my two-year-old son Benjamin. At the same time, I had been reading a science magazine about the possibility of using liquid crystal displays (LCDs) to produce tiny, flat color TV screens."

**The MARK is Ready**

The continuity of the two thoughts lit the proverbial light bulb. Why not, he thought, devise a helmet with an LCD in front of each eye, generating a moving version of the stereo-slide viewer? Add synchronized three dimensional sound, using Seinheiser sound system, and—virtual reality.

The existing Seinheiser system was developed in Germany to replace stereo sound, which is produced by recording sounds entering the left and right sides of a microphone. The Germans, realizing that we hear the world in 360 degrees sound, rather than simple stereo, concluded that this is because the sound waves entering the left ear are slightly different from those entering the right, broken up by the skull, hair, nose, ears, etc.

The Seinheiser system, however, uses an artificial head with the acoustic properties of the human skull, placing high quality headphones where the eardrums would be. When sound recorded that way was played back, it fooled the brain into thinking it was hearing the real world.

Although it was a significant advance, Seinheiser's system could only be experienced through headphones, says Gale, and never took off, remaining of interest only to dedicated audiophiles.

Gales told some friends about his idea to create an alternative reality combining these audiovisual elements, but no one paid much attention. Determined to push it, he commissioned the building of a prototype using two video cameras and LCD screens and two microphones.

**The MARK is Ready**

"I was working on scientific publications at a $1-billion telecommunications company in Toronto. An engineer there cobbled together a first, proof-of-concept prototype, but his about-to-retire boss declared: "Humph! Just a fad!"

Gale then spent a year talking to numerous engineers in the fields of physics, optics, broadcasting and electronics (each conversation protected by a non-disclosure document) to determine the viability of the concept as a means of mass entertainment.

The following year, 1984, he applied to the U.S. patent office after reading a book on how to patent your own invention. "A clerk called, told me the idea could be very big, and suggested I was only shooting myself in the foot by not seeking out the best legal help available."

Gale then retained the best patent attorneys in Canada, who found that a man named Helig had patented something similar to his idea in 1962. But he had used black-and-white cathode ray tubes, like those in TV sets, in front of the eyes on the helmet.

"Their use in a helmet would have been dangerous" says Gale. "Also his reliance on simple stereo sound would have maintained a distance between the

**The MARK is Ready**

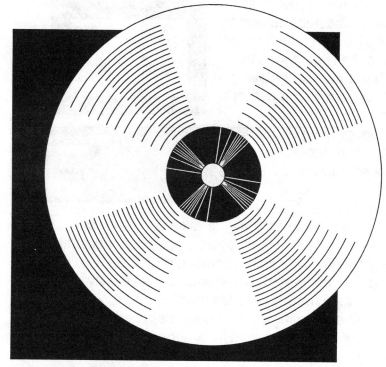

programming and the viewer, interfering with the virtually real feel of the experience. He never renewed the
patent when it ran out 17 years later, and the idea was
never commercialized."

Gale's lawyers filed a second, more professionally-
worded application, but the patent office was concerned
that his idea was too close to Helig's to justify a new
patent.

"The struggle was to convince Washington that the
combination of a safe-to-watch, moving, color 3-D

**The MARK is Ready**

image with synchronized, 3-D sound represented a qualitative, rather than quantitative difference."

With only one shot left at the patent (the U.S. Patent Office allows only three attempts before rejecting an application for good), Gale decided to hedge his bets by adding something incontrovertibly new; a custom-designed scent-generating component. So he sat down and invented a way to produce artificial scents that could be released automatically in coordination with a particular scene viewed through the LCDs.

He used a sphere, similar to the ball once used on IBM typewriters, with tiny scent pellets instead of raised letters. When hit, the spot could produce an odor—from the pleasant smell or roses to the unpleasant whiff of a garbage dump. A tiny fan inside the helmet would spread the scent when required, and cool the viewer's eyes in their light-tight goggles at other times.

Although film technology was relatively primitive in the early 80's, Gale conceived even then of the possibility of filming in a 180-degree semicircle to expand the view in the helmet. This is easily done today. He also suggested his invention's potential use as a simulator for medical, military, and exploratory uses, and the possible use of computer sources to generate images. "A pilot could sit in a room somewhere and release a bomb from a non-piloted jet over an enemy country" he says.

Also in 1984, Gale first wrote to the Sony Corporation in Japan, suggesting his idea. "They wrote back saying sorry, the technology for virtual reality was

**The MARK is Ready**

not yet available." Since then, Sony's intellectual property division has written to acknowledge his patent, but says the company has no intention of marketing "this idea in this market (the U.S.) at this time."

Sony is currently selling VR helmets in Japan and Europe, but has kept out of the U.S. as required by the patent. "I have seen no signs" says Gale, "that Sony intends to violate the patent restrictions on sales there."

In August 1990, Gale was awarded U.S. Patent No. 4,952,024 by the U.S. Patent Office. "It cost $12,000 all told. If I had had another $50,000, I would have been able to register the patent throughout the world, giving me royalties on all VR helmets sold anywhere. But I couldn't afford it" he recalls regretfully. In any case, the U.S. where his patent is in effect will comprise the major VR market.

Unlike Sony, at least two other companies—Sega and Nintendo—are charging ahead without considering Gale's patent. When he learned of their intention to market VR games in the U.S. for entertainment purposes this winter, he wrote to inform them he held the patent, and invited them to apply for a license. "They didn't bother even to respond" he recalls.

Gale soon realized that despite the fact that the law was on his side, he would have difficulty fighting billion-dollar corporations without some high-powered defenders. He found his way to a large Israeli corporation, which is carrying out serious negotiations with him. "I figured that if I offered them some of the potential income, they would agree to finance the fight against

**The MARK is Ready**

violators of the patent." Although this company had never been involved in such an arrangement, they are discussing the possibility of providing the Israeli inventor with a financial stick in his fight for royalties. "I was looking for a company with resources to pursue a lawsuit to the bitter end. Also, I wanted some of the benefit of the idea to come to Israel" Gale says.

As for the hoped-for change in his bank balance, Gale says he and his wife "try not to think about it. We're too busy trying to make ends meet."

Deuteronomy 28:1–13 reads as follows,

*"And it shall come to pass, if thou shalt hearken diligently unto the voice of the LORD thy God, to observe and to do all his commandments which I command thee this day, that the LORD thy God will set thee on high above all nations of the earth: And all these blessings shall come on thee, and overtake thee, if thou shalt hearken unto the voice of the LORD thy God. Blessed shalt thou be in the city, and blessed shalt thou be in the field. Blessed shall be the fruit of thy body, and the fruit of thy ground, and the fruit of thy cattle, the increase of thy kine, and the flocks of thy sheep. Blessed shall be thy basket and thy store. Blessed shalt thou be when thou comest in, and blessed shalt thou be when thou goest out. The LORD shall cause thine enemies that rise up against thee to be smitten before thy face: they shall come out against thee*

**The MARK is Ready**

*one way, and flee before thee seven ways. The LORD shall command the blessing upon thee in thy storehouses, and in all that thou settest thine hand unto; and he shall bless thee in the land which the LORD thy God giveth thee. The LORD shall establish thee an holy people unto himself, as he hath sworn unto thee, if thou shalt keep the commandments of the LORD thy God, and walk in his ways. And all people of the earth shall see that thou art called by the name of the LORD; and they shall be afraid of thee. And the LORD shall make thee plenteous in goods, in the fruit of thy body, and in the fruit of thy cattle, and in the fruit of thy ground, in the land which the LORD sware unto thy fathers to give thee. The LORD shall open unto thee his good treasure, the heaven to give the rain unto thy land in his season, and to bless all the work of thine hand: and thou shalt lend unto many nations, and thou shalt not borrow. And the LORD shall make thee the head, and not the tail; and thou shalt be above only, and thou shalt not be beneath; if that thou hearken unto the commandments of the LORD thy God, which I command thee this day, to observe and to do them."*

And we also read in Deuteronomy 32:8–9,

*"When the Most High divided to the nations their inheritance, when he separated the sons of Adam, he set the bounds of the people according to the number of the children of Israel. For the*

**The MARK is Ready**

*LORD'S portion is his people; Jacob is the lot of his inheritance."*

I'll never forget my first virtual reality "trip." I suited up for the experience by donning a pair of video goggles and a glove wired to pick up my finger movements. A headset-mounted device tracked my body position.

My "coach" explained that I would use hand signals to move around in the three-dimensional world I saw through the goggles. By pointing my index finger at objects, I could fly toward them. To grasp objects, I would curl my fingers around them. A disembodied hand mirrored the movements of my real hand and marked my place in the computer simulation.

The virtual world I stepped into looked nothing like the real world I had left behind. There were only a few, simple objects in sight. I saw a swimming pool, a rubber duck, a top hat floating in mid-air, and a red tower. When I grabbed the hat, it disappeared. My coach laughed. "It's a magic hat," he explained.

He told me to look up, and I saw a fluffy cloud "If you point at it, you can go up inside it" he said. So I zoomed up into the cloud, where I was immediately surrounded by gray fog. I came out a moment later and flew away.

Suddenly my coach, who had been talking with someone else in the room, glanced at a monitor

**The MARK is Ready**

that showed him what I saw seeing. "Uh-oh!" he said. "Usually we put a ceiling on our worlds, so you can't go too high. But we just created this world last night, and we didn't have time to add the ceiling.

"You're way up in the sky," he said. "See that dot there?" he asked, turning me toward it. "That's the tower. Point your finger at it, so you can fly back down there."

I aimed at the speck, and it began to grow larger. I was speeding toward the ground, diving faster than a hawk after a rabbit. Sweat beaded up on my forehead, and the muscles in my gut clenched into the sort of knot that forms when you're in the front seat of a roller coaster with your hands over your head. The virtual simulation was so overwhelming that I did not notice my ears weren't popping and my feet were planted firmly on the floor.

I landed by the swimming pool and peeled off the goggles. As I looked around at the real world, I had a new appreciation for its rich detail—and for my own suggestibility.

Using virtual reality to interface with complex data is another target for developers. Consider a stock fund manager responsible for tracking the performance of thousands of companies around the world.

Rather than dealing with text or flat graphs, developer Maxus Systems International in New

**The MARK is Ready**

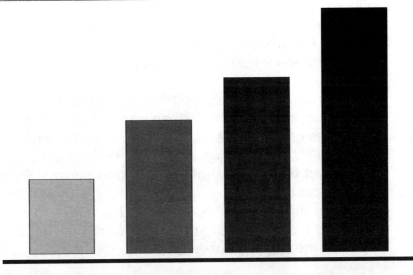

York displays information dynamically in a spatially arranged world.

Imagine circling the equivalent of Manhattan Island in a helicopter with the ability to swoop down for a closer view of individual skyscrapers. The buildings are actually 3-D bar graphs that sport corporate logos.

The stock values, and particular stocks can be clustered in neighborhoods by industry or continent. Blinkers and spinners can be added to the tops of the bars to attract attention if, for example, the value of a stock starts to fall.

If you get lost in space, the cyberspace equivalent of navigating into the non-graphics void, a double tetrahedral icon with a female voice named LIA (for Limited Intelligent Agent) can be called upon to lead you back to populated cyberspace.

## The MARK is Ready

## Neural Aerobics

Psalm 90: 9-12 reads as follows,

> *"For all our days are passed away in thy wrath: we spend our years as a tale that is told. The days of our years are threescore years and ten; and if by reason of strength they be fourscore years, yet is their strength labour and sorrow; for it is soon cut off, and we fly away. Who knoweth the power of thine anger? even according to thy fear, so is thy wrath. So teach us to number our days, that we may apply our hearts unto wisdom."*

And now we turn to the November, 1993 edition of *Popular Science,*

"Fortunately, the realism of virtual reality is improving all the time. For those who might have been turned off by the low resolution of *Dactyl Nightmare*, there's a more sophisticated alternative based on the television series, *Star Trek: The Next Generation*. Called *StarPost*, it's due to open later this year. A lighter-weight HMD will offer triple the number of pixels and a wider view. You will enter a transporter room and use the HMD as a means to beam down to a planet. Spectrum Holobyte, a computer games company in Alameda, California, is

**The MARK is Ready**

developing the software. A key component is a powerful computer called the Reality Engine from Silicon Graphics, which makes high-end workstations. (In contrast, each *Dactyl Nightmare* station is run from an Amiga computer). A more ambitious 30,000-square-foot facility, called *United Federation of Planets: Star Base*, is also planned, Halliday says *Star Base* won't open until the end of 1994.

"Virtual reality is where personal computers were in 1979" declares Ben Delaney, editor and publisher of *Cyberedge Journal*, a newsletter based in Sausalito, California. "PCs back then were slow. They didn't do much. They crashed a lot. But you could start to see the promise. Ten years later everything was changed. Virtual reality may have a little longer gestation period, but it has the same potential."

1st Corinthians 1:25–28 tells us,

*"Because the foolishness of God is wiser than men; and the weakness of God is stronger than men. For ye see your calling, brethren, how that not many wise men after the flesh, not many mighty, not many noble, are called: But God hath chosen the foolish things of the world to confound the wise; and God hath chosen the weak things of the world to confound the things which are mighty; And base things of the world, and things which are despised, hath God chosen, yea, and things which are not, to bring to nought things that are."*

**The MARK is Ready**

Now, I am quoting from *Popular Science*, June 1993, where an article entitled, "Computer With Humanlike Brains" caught my attention:

"No computer can match the processing power of the human brain, but Intel Corp. and Nestor Inc. believe they've come much closer to that human ideal with a more advanced "neural network" chip they recently delivered to the government's Defense Advanced Research Projects Agency, or DARPA.

The new chip, called the Ni1000, has 1,024 artificial neurons. That's puny compared with the more than 100 billion neurons typical of a human brain.

But with much fewer neurons, those 1,024 stand-ins can operate roughly 10,000 times faster than their biological equivalents, using electrons to transmit information instead of the sodium and potassium ions required by the human brain.

Like the brain, the Ni1000 "learns" and is particularly adept at pattern recognition, recognizing objects and shapes among the millions of bits of data that pass through it.

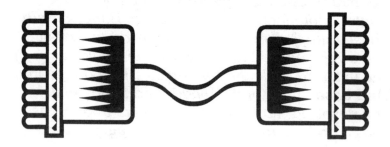

**The MARK is Ready**

That makes the Ni1000 well-suited for applications such as military target recognition, collision avoidance systems, and forms processing. Nestor Inc., the Providence, Rhode Island company that wrote the chip's built-in software, estimates that the Ni1000 could improve the character-recognition capabilities of a computer by the orders of magnitude, from 10 to 10,000 characters per second.

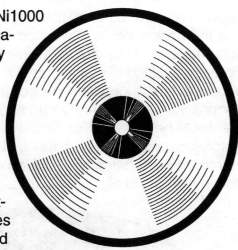

Later this year, Intel says the Ni1000 should be available on add-in boards for PCs that use its 486 or Pentium microprocessors. Such additions may cost as much as the PC itself, however."

### Hold that Thought: Computers Read Minds!

Someday, the latest wave in computers may be brain waves. In separate projects, computer scientists in both the United States and Japan are investigating what many call the ultimate interface between man and machine: human thought.

In the United States, researchers are using several approaches to developing thought-controlled computers. At the New York state Department of Health in Albany, researchers are "training" users to emit brain signals that tell a computer to move a cursor around the screen. Psychologists at the University of Illinois have developed a kind of mind-controlled typewriter, enabling people to type by spelling out words in their minds (though very slowly). And in yet another experiment at the Smith-Kewttlewell Eye Research Institute in San Francisco, researchers are using electrical signals from an electroencephalogram in which electrodes are attached to the scalp, to tell where a person is looking

**The MARK is Ready**

on a computer screen.

In Japan, a joint group of researchers from Fujitsu Ltd. and Hokkaido University in Atsugi are focusing on the region of the human brain that generates "silent speech" or the conception of a syllable before it is actually voiced. To track the brain waves to the silent speech center at the front of the brain, the heads of test subjects are fitted with 12 electrodes. In a recent demonstration, researchers were able to determine accurately when test subjects thought the sound "oh" in response to a randomly flashed light. The next step is a series of experiments to see if they can distinguish between a silent "yes" and "no" using a more sensitive *superconducting quantum interference device*, or SQUID, to track brain waves.

The key to all of these efforts is the fact that the human brain emits electrical signals in varying voltages just before an action is performed. Computer scientists attempt to perceive patterns in these signals and match them with specific actions. In many cases, that requires

**The MARK is Ready**

training users to channel or control their thoughts as well. How far any measuring device can probe into the complex mental map of the brain, and how much control we can exert over the way we think, remain daunting mysteries, however.

Eventually, these experiments could lead to a general-purpose interface that supplements, or even replaces, keyboards and speech-recognition systems. But researchers warn that a true mind-control computer may be decades away."

Psalm 139:14–16 tells the psalmist's thankful refrain of how God has put us together,

*"I will praise thee; for I am fearfully and won-derfully made: marvellous are thy works; and that my soul knoweth right well. My substance was not hid from thee, when I was made in secret, and curiously wrought in the lowest parts of the earth Thine eyes did see my substance, yet being unper-fect; and in thy book all my members were written, which in continuance were fashioned, when as yet there was none of them."* ■

**The MARK is Ready**

# EPILOGUE

This book has intended to show how near we are to the end of this age, and that everything is being made ready for the Antichrist system.

The *mark* and *number* are incorporated in the Universal Product Code that perfectly fits the description of marks and numbers given in Revelation 13, verses 15 through 18. The barcode will become the international means of commerce and trade and encompass everything involved in global traffic.

The microchip will make "people control" a dreaded reality and will doubtless bear the logo (666) of the beast.

The birth of the Internet will successfully tie together global telecommunications, and the *soul* of Internet may well be synonymous with the Image of the Beast spoken of in Revelation 13:15!

Virtual Reality will become commonplace and may well help some individuals to survive the tribulation period of 7 years. However, it may well be one of the major tools by which the Antichrist deceives the whole world.

May God use *The Mark is Ready* to help many people to better understand the endtime scenario, and that the imminency of Christ's soon-return is truly our *blessed hope*!

—Dr. David Webber

**The MARK is Ready**

**Special offer!**
**Just $15 for 1 year!**
**12 issues packed with color!**